NICK JR

DORA the EXPLORER

PHONICS
READING PROGRAM

W9-BNI-507

(Books 7-12)

On the Go!

Dora's Showtime! · I Missed You! · Dora Saves the Game
Dora Takes a Hike · At the Beach · Snowy Day

SCHOLASTIC INC.
New York   Toronto   London   Auckland   Sydney
Mexico City   New Delhi   Hong Kong   Buenos Aires

Dora the Explorer™: Dora's Showtime! (0-439-67762-9) © 2004 Viacom International Inc.
Dora the Explorer™: I Missed You! (0-439-67763-7) © 2004 Viacom International Inc.
Dora the Explorer™: Dora Saves the Game (0-439-67764-5) © 2004 Viacom International Inc.
Dora the Explorer™: Dora Takes a Hike (0-439-67765-3) © 2004 Viacom International Inc.
Dora the Explorer™: At the Beach (0-439-67766-1) © 2004 Viacom International Inc.
Dora the Explorer™: Snowy Day (0-439-67767-X) © 2004 Viacom International Inc.

NICKELODEON, NICK JR., Dora the Explorer, and all related titles, logos, and characters are trademarks of Viacom International Inc. All rights reserved.

Used under license by Scholastic Inc. Published by Scholastic Inc. SCHOLASTIC and associated logos are trademarks and/or registered trademarks of Scholastic Inc.

ISBN-13: 978-0-439-90238-0
ISBN-10: 0-439-90238-X

12 11 10 9 8 7 6 5 4 3   7 8 9 10 11/0

Printed in the U.S.A.
This compilation edition first printing, September 2006

Welcome to **Dora the Explorer's** Phonics Reading Program!

Learning to read is so important for your child's success in school and in life. Now **Dora the Explorer** is here to help your child learn important phonics skills. Here's how the following six stories work:

Take phonics, the fundamental skill of knowing that the letters we read represent the sounds we hear and say. Add **Dora** and help your child LEARN to read and LOVE to read!

To be a good reader, it takes practice. That's where **Dora the Explorer** can make a difference. Kids love **Dora** and will want to read her latest adventures over and over again. Try these ideas for enjoying the books with your child:

- Read together by taking turns line by line or page by page.

- Look for all the words that have the sound being featured in the reader. Read them over and over again.

- Have your child read the story to you and then retell it in his or her own words.

Scholastic has been helping families encourage young readers for more than 80 years. Thank you for letting us help you support your beginning reader.

Happy reading,

Francie Alexander,
Chief Academic Officer, Scholastic Inc.

In this story, you can learn all about the "ch," "sh," "th," and "wh" sounds. Here are some words to sound out.

ch	sh	th	wh
chair	shake	the	when
check	shine	them	where
chicken	show	they	whistle

These are words that you will see in this story and many other stories. You will want to learn them as well.

our **out** **think** **who**

These are some more challenging words that you will see in this story.

feather	grand	special
finish	loud	tunes

NICK JR

DORA
the
EXPLORER

PHONICS
READING PROGRAM

Book 7
sh, ch
th, wh

Dora's Showtime!

by Quinlan B. Lee

SCHOLASTIC INC.

New York Toronto London Auckland Sydney
Mexico City New Delhi Hong Kong Buenos Aires

Welcome to
Fiesta Theatre!
Grab a chair!
It is showtime!
Our first star loves
his shiny boots and
shaking his maracas.

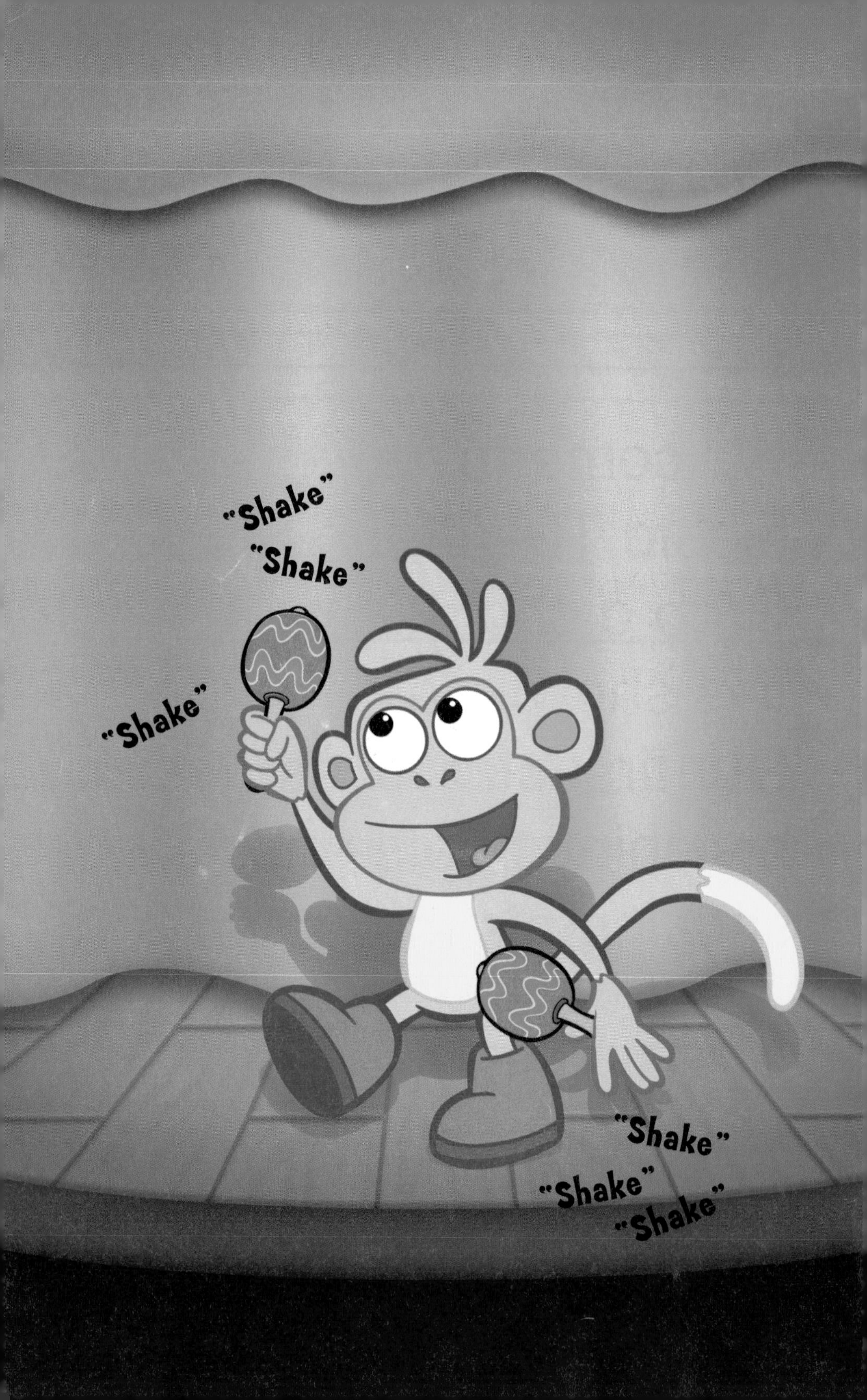
"Shake"
"Shake"
"Shake"
"Shake"
"Shake"
"Shake"

There he is!
Show them how you
shake to the beat, Boots!
Good job!
Next out are three friends.
They play together
wherever they go.
Do you know
who they are?

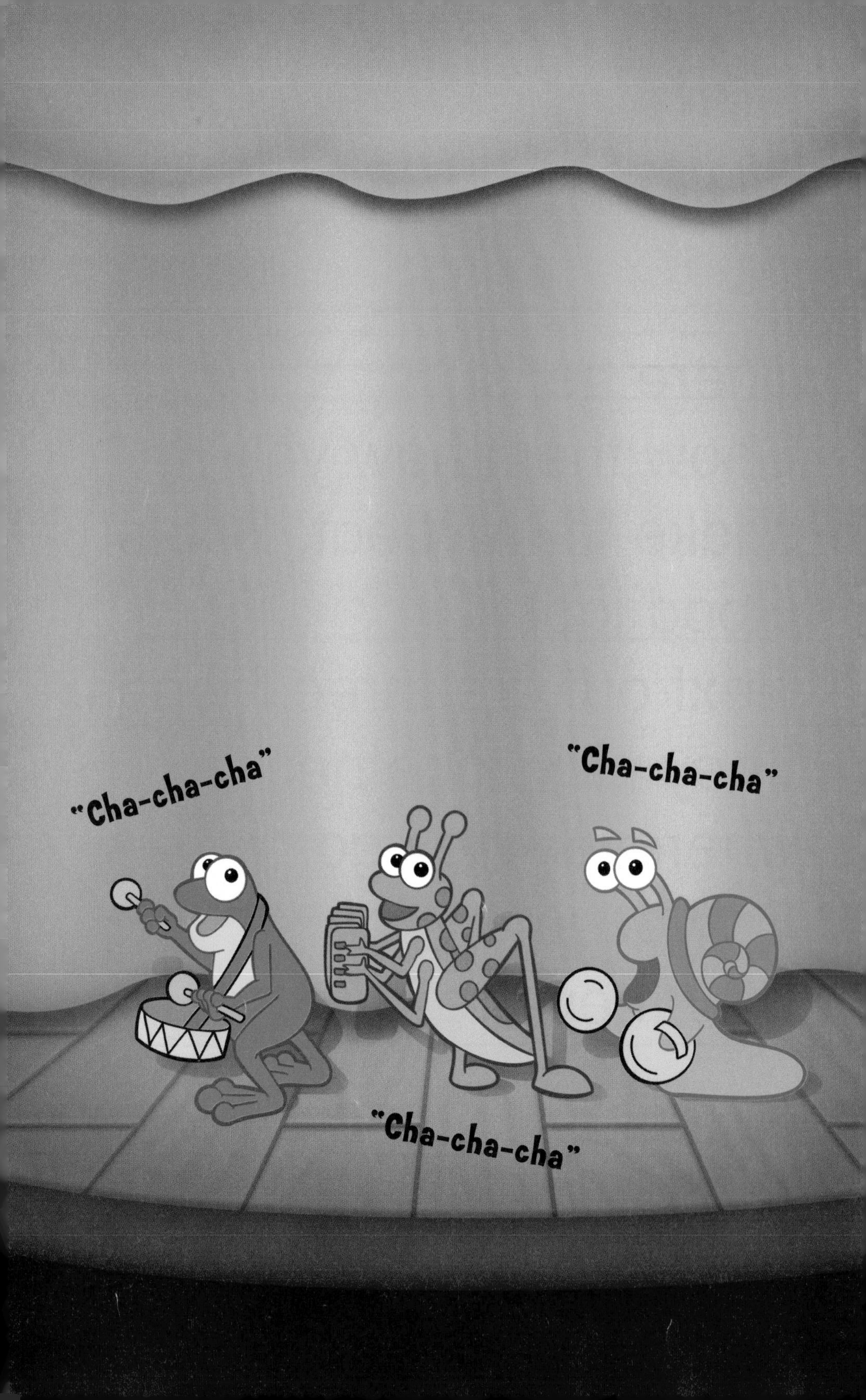
"Cha-cha-cha"
"Cha-cha-cha"
"Cha-cha-cha"

Give a whistle
for the Fiesta Trio!
They are here
to play a cha-cha.
They love to play
their tunes
come rain or shine.

Next up is . . . uh-oh.
Stop the show!
Where is our next star?
Shhh . . .
I think I hear him.
*Chugga-Chugga-
Choo-Choo!*
Do you know who it is?

That's right!
It is Azul with his
shiny new whistle.
Whoo-Whoo!
Time for the next act.
When he is not at the farm
he likes to thump his drum
and shout a song.

Check out Benny,
the bongo bull!
Show them how it's done,
Benny!
And for our grand finish
we have a special treat.

The Big Red Chicken
will teach us how to do
his catchy chicken dance.
Come on!
Shake a tail feather
and *bawk* out loud!

Thanks for coming
to our show!

In this story, you can learn all about plurals.
Here are some words to sound out.

days   **nuts**

flowers   **times**

gifts   **trees**

These are words that you will see in this story
and many other stories. You will want to learn
them as well.

her   **many**   **one**   **three**

These are some more challenging words that
you will see in this story.

count   **minutes**   **should**

house   **missed**   **visit**

NICK JR.

DORA the EXPLORER

PHONICS
READING PROGRAM

I Missed You!

by Quinlan B. Lee

SCHOLASTIC INC.

New York   Toronto   London   Auckland   Sydney
Mexico City   New Delhi   Hong Kong   Buenos Aires

My Abuela is coming
to visit today.
I haven't seen her
for three whole days!
I want to give her
three gifts to show her
that I missed her.
Will you help me?

Abuela loves flowers.
Let's pick some for her.
I want to pick five flowers.
One, two, three, four, five.

That's one gift.
How many more gifts
do we need?
Right!
We need two more gifts.
I know Abuela loves nuts.
Where could we find her
some nuts?

Tico's Tree!
Wow!
Look at all these nuts.
Tico, can we have
some nuts for Abuela?
Count four from the tree.
One, two, three, four.

Oh, no!
We have to go.
Abuela will be at
my house
in less
than five minutes.
How can we get there
in time?

Tico's car!
Thanks, Tico.
Wait, what's in
those trees?
It is Swiper.
He wants to swipe
the gifts.
Quick, say,
"Swiper, no swiping"
three times.
We did it!

Hooray!
Abuela's here!
But we need one
more gift.
What should it be?

A hug from me!
I missed you, Abuela!

In this story, you can learn all about the long "a" sound. Here are some words to sound out.

bay   **race**

game   **save**

play   **wait**

These are words that you will see in this story and many other stories. You will want to learn them as well.

but   could   place   where

These are some more challenging words that you will see in this story.

change   **cousin**   **might**

clouds   **idea**   **soccer**

DORA the EXPLORER

PHONICS
READING PROGRAM

Dora Saves the Game

by Quinlan B. Lee

SCHOLASTIC INC.

New York   Toronto   London   Auckland   Sydney

Mexico City   New Delhi   Hong Kong   Buenos Aires

It has been wet
and gray for days.

My cousin, Diego,
came to play.
He wants to play
a game of soccer.
There is no dry place
to play here.
Where else could
we play?

Boots says to play
by the bay.
But a wave might spray
and wash the ball away.
We need a new place
to play.

Diego says that
we could play
far away in the hills.
Maybe the clouds will not
chase us there.

Way to go, Diego.
This is a dry place.
Let's play!

Oh, no!
The ball won't stay.
We must race to save it.
This is no way to play.
We must change places.

Wait!
Diego gave me an idea.
Play Park!
It is away from the gray
and in the sun's rays.

This is a great place.
We saved the game.

In this story, you can learn all about the long "i" sound. Here are some words to sound out.

find   **life**

hike   **sky**

high   **while**

These are words that you will see in this story and many other stories. You will want to learn them as well.

a   **down**   **like**   **right**

These are some more challenging words that you will see in this story.

boat   **mountain**   **river**

climb   **outside**   **tired**

PHONICS
READING PROGRAM

Dora Takes a Hike

by Quinlan B. Lee

SCHOLASTIC INC.
New York   Toronto   London   Auckland   Sydney
Mexico City   New Delhi   Hong Kong   Buenos Aires

Hi! Let's go outside.
The sun is high.
The sky is blue.
What a fine day
to take a hike!

We hiked to the river.
It is wide and on the rise.
How can we get
to the other side?
Right!
We can ride in the boat.
But we need
our life jackets.

Do you spy Swiper?
Where is he hiding?
Can we say, "Swiper,
no swiping" in time?

Oh, no!
Swiper swiped
our life jackets!
He tossed them up high.
We have to climb
the vines.
Did you find them?
Good spying!
Now let's get
to the other side.

Boots and I like to hike
up Tallest Mountain.
It is a little while away.
We can find it by two other
high mountains.
Then we can climb!

This part of our hike
takes us high
up in the sky.
Do you spy
some birds flying by?
One, two, three, four, five!

We did it!
We climbed Tallest
Mountain!
I like to hike,
but I am tired.
Look!
A slide we can ride
down the other side.

That hike was nice.
See you next time!

In this story, you can learn all about the long "e" sound. Here are some words to sound out.

keep	**sea**
meet	**knees**
neat	**we**

These are words that you will see in this story and many other stories. You will want to learn them as well.

be   **on**   **see**   **what**

These are some more challenging words that you will see in this story.

beach	**breeze**	**seashell**
creep	**seagull**	**starfish**

PHONICS
READING PROGRAM

At the Beach

by Quinlan B. Lee

SCHOLASTIC INC.

New York   Toronto   London   Auckland   Sydney
Mexico City   New Delhi   Hong Kong   Buenos Aires

Boots and I are
at the beach.
It is a nice day
to be by the sea.
I love to lean back
and feel the breeze.

I like to feel the sand
on my knees.
Hey, do you see what's
creeping in the sand?
Pleased to meet you,
Mister Crab!

What does Boots
have under his seashell?
Let's take a peek!
It is a neat starfish!

Wait!
Did you see something
speed by?
What could it be?
Was it a speedboat?
Or maybe a seagull?

No!
It was Swiper!
He swiped Boots'
seashell.
Did he keep it?
No, he tossed it
out to sea.

How can we reach it?
We need a rope.
Do you see one?
Me neither.
What do you see nearby?

The reeds!
Great idea!
We can use these.
Then if we creep out
on the pier,
we can reach
the seashell.

We did it!

In this story, you can learn all about the long "o" sound. Here are some words to sound out.

cold   **home**

blows   **slow**

froze   **snow**

These are words that you will see in this story and many other stories. You will want to learn them as well.

do   **old**   **over**   **so**

These are some more challenging words that you will see in this story.

answer   **marshmallows**   **road**

chocolate   **riddle**   **skating**

PHONICS
READING PROGRAM

Snowy Day

by Quinlan B. Lee

SCHOLASTIC INC.

New York   Toronto   London   Auckland   Sydney
Mexico City   New Delhi   Hong Kong   Buenos Aires

It is a snowy day!
It is so cold that
the river froze.
We can go skating.

Whoa!
It is so slippery!
We need to go slow
so we don't fall down.
Uh-oh!
Hold on, Boots!
I'm coming.

Whew!
That was close.
We both almost fell.
Brrrr.
When the wind blows
I am cold.
Let's go home.

Oh, no!
Map shows that
the road home
goes over the Grumpy Old
Troll's Bridge.
I hope we know
the answer to his riddle.

Grumpy Old Troll says,
"It starts up high
and falls down low,
in between it swirls
and blows.
What is it?
Do you know?"

Right!
It is snow!
Way to go!
The troll let us go over.
Come on!
This snowy road
will take us home.

We made it.
It is so warm at home
by the stove.
Mom made hot chocolate
and marshmallows.
Mmm.

I love snow!
But I also love coming home!